FISH
FOR
SUPPER!

Written by Morgan Matthews
Illustrated by Susan Miller

Troll Associates

Library of Congress Cataloging in Publication Data

Matthews, Morgan.
  Fish for supper!

    Summary: Carl Cat sets out to catch a fish for
supper but has a change of heart.
    [1. Cats—Fiction. 2. Fishing—Fiction] I. Miller,
Susan, 1956-   ill. II. Title.
PZ7.M43425Fi   1986   [E]   85-14056
ISBN 0-8167-0588-7 (lib. bdg.)
ISBN 0-8167-0589-5 (pbk.)

10   9   8   7   6   5   4   3   2

The Homestead School
2100 Hollow Road
Glen Spey, NY 12737

FISH
FOR
SUPPER!

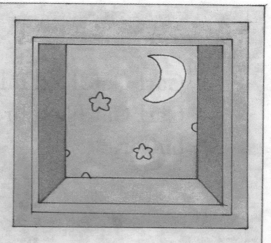

What do you like to have for supper? Do you like milk? Do you like bread with butter?

Carl Cat liked milk.
Carl Cat liked bread with
butter.

Carl Cat had a good supper every day. He had milk. He had bread with butter. Every day Carl had milk and buttered bread.

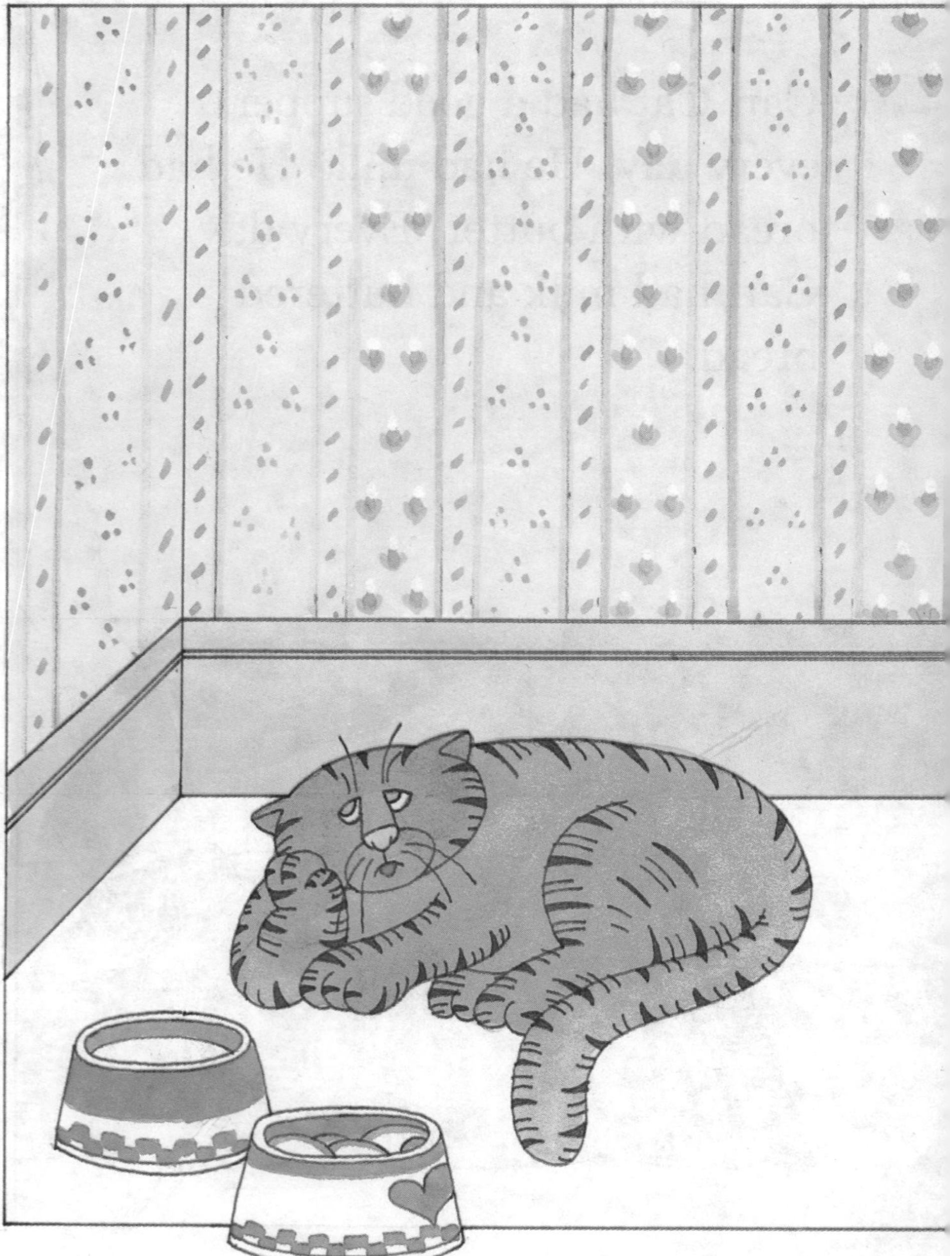

Carl's supper was good. But every day it was the same. Supper got dull.

"Yuch!" said Carl. "Supper is dull. A dull supper is not a good supper. I want something new." What is good for a cat's supper?

"Fish!" cried Carl. "Cats like fish. And it is something new. I will have fish for supper."

Carl Cat wanted to have fish. But where can a cat get fish? "There are fish in the lake," said Carl. "I will go fishing. I will catch a fish for supper."

Carl Cat put on fishing boots.
He got a fishing pole. He put
fishing line on the pole. On the
line he put a fishhook.

The cat looked at the pole. He
looked at the fishing line. Then
he looked at the hook.
"This will catch a fish," he said.
"All I need is one more thing."

Away went Carl Cat in his big
boots. Away he went to get one
more thing. What thing?
Worms! Squirmy, wiggly worms!

To fish, you need worms. Fish
like worms that wiggle. And
Carl wanted to catch a fish.

Carl went looking for worms. He
looked here. He looked there.
"Oh, worms!" cried Carl.
"Squirmy, wiggly worms! Where
are you?"

The cat saw some worms. The worms saw Carl. Away the worms wiggled. They did not want to go fishing. Fish like worms. But worms do not like fish.

The worms wiggled and
wiggled. But they did not get
away. Carl caught the worms.
He did not want to hurt them.
But he needed worms to fish.

"Now I can go fishing," said
Carl. "I have everything I need.
I have a fishing pole, fishing
line, a hook, and wiggly
worms."

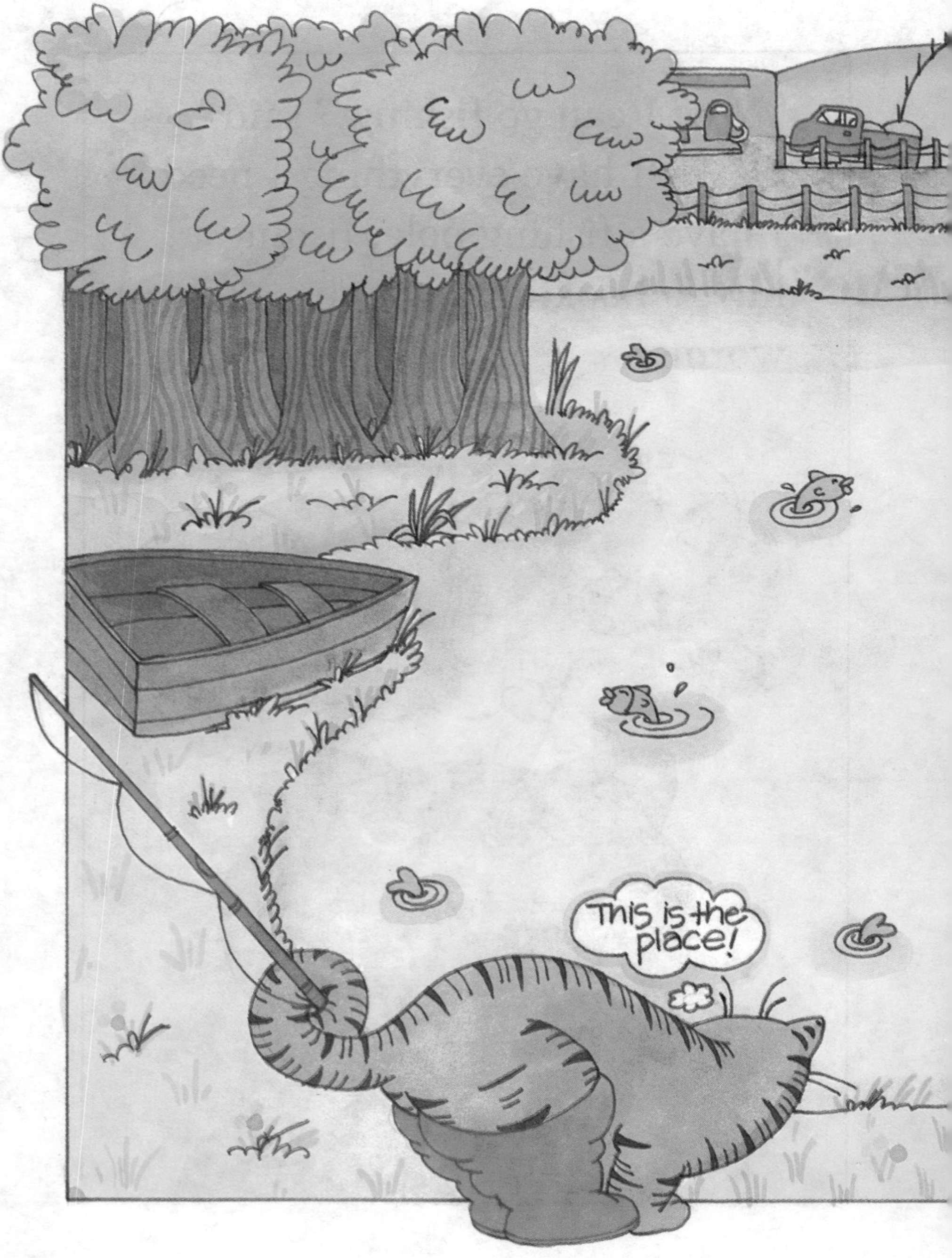
This is the place!

Carl went to the lake. He looked
for a good place. He wanted a
place with lots of fish.
"How about this place?" said
Carl.

Carl looked in the lake. He saw
fish. He saw little fish. He saw
big fish. Oh, what a lot of fish.
"This is the place!" cried Carl.

"Fish for supper!" he cried. "Fish
in the lake!"
Carl jumped up and down.
Oh-oh. Look out, Carl! Now
there's a cat in the lake, too!

Away went the little fish. Away went the big fish.

"Yuch!" cried Carl. "A lake is good for a fish. It is not good for a cat."

Carl climbed out of the lake.

"Now I will fish," said he. "I will put a worm on my hook. I will put the line in the lake. My pole will catch a fish."

Carl took out a worm. The worm wiggled and wiggled. It did not want to go on the hook. A hook hurts. Oh, does a hook hurt!

Carl looked at the worm. He looked at the hook. Carl was a good cat. He did not like to hurt things.

"I cannot hurt you, little worm,"
cried Carl. "I cannot put you on
a hook. I will catch a fish
without wiggly worms."

The cat let the worms go. Away they went.

"My worms are gone," said Carl. "But I still want a fish for supper. I do not want supper to be dull."

Carl was going to fish. He looked
at the fishhook.
"Oh, a hook must hurt," he said.
"I want to catch a fish. But I do
not want to hurt a fish."

What to do? Hooks hurt fish.
Hooks hurt worms. How could a
good cat fish?

"The tip of the hook hurts," said
Carl. "Without the tip, the hook
is dull."
Off went the tip!
"A dull hook will not hurt," said
Carl. "But will it catch a fish?"

31

The cat went fishing. In the lake
went the fishing line. In went
the dull hook. What a way to
fish!

Carl fished here. He did not
catch a fish.

Carl fished there. He did not
catch a fish.

"Fishing can be a little dull," said Carl. "Where are all the fish?"

Carl fished at a new place. He
fished. And he fished.
"What a day!" he cried. "Will I
ever catch anything?"

Then Carl's fishing line wiggled.
His fishing pole wiggled.
"Oh-oh," cried Carl. "Is
something on my hook?"

Out of the lake went the line! What was on the hook? What did Carl catch? Was it a big fish?

It was not a fish.
"It's a big boot!" said Carl. "I caught a fishing boot. What a catch!"

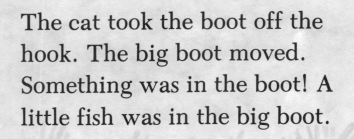

The cat took the boot off the
hook. The big boot moved.
Something was in the boot! A
little fish was in the big boot.

"A fish!" cried Carl. "I will have a fish for supper!"

"Supper?" said the fish. "Can I have supper with you? Supper in the lake is always the same. It is dull. Every day I have worms. Wiggly worms for supper! I'm tired of them."

The cat looked at the fish. He could not hurt the fish.
"I will not have a fish for supper," said Carl. "I will have a fish *to* supper."

"What is for supper?" said the
fish.
"We will have milk in a bowl,"
said Carl. "And we will have
buttered bread."

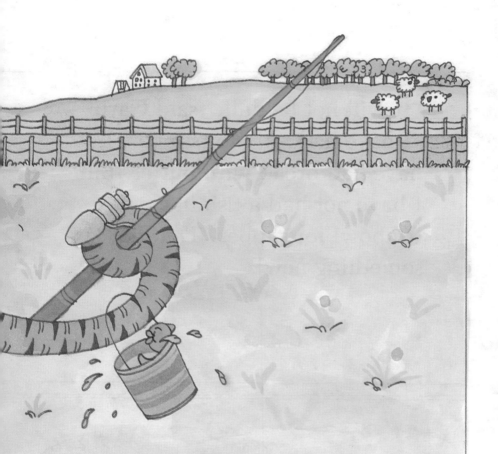

"I do not like milk in a bowl,"
said the fish. "But I like bread. It
will be a good supper."

"It will not be dull," said Carl. "I have had milk for supper. I have had bread with butter. But I have not had a fish in a fishbowl for supper. That is something new!"

That day supper was very good.
Carl had bread and butter. He
had milk in a bowl. And he had
something new. He had a fish in
a fishbowl.

What did the fish have? He had bread without butter.

What do you like to have for supper?

FISH